DESTINATION MONTREAL

by Janice Hamilton

Lerner Publications Company • Minneapolis

PHOTO ACKNOWLEDGMENTS
Cover photo by Yves Marcoux/Tony Stone Images. All inside photos by © Robert Holmes, pp. 5, 20, 64, 65 (bottom), 76; Don Eastman Photo, pp.6, 20-21; The Port of Montreal, pp. 9, 12, 14 (top), 17 (top), 22 (both), 48, 52, 60, 61, 74-75; Louis-Michel Major, pp. 13, 14 (bottom), 24, 25, 55; courtesy of St. Lawrence Seaway Authority, Ottawa, Ontario, p. 17 (bottom); courtesy of St. Lawrence Seaway Authority, Cornwall, Ontario, p. 19 (top); courtesy of Fisheries and Oceans, Quebec City, Quebec, p. 19 (bottom); McCord Museum of Canadian History, Notman Photographic Archives, pp. 26, 37 (both), 39 (both), 41; © Wolfgang Kaehler, pp. 51, 62, 70 (top); The Stewart Museum at the Fort, Île Sainte-Hélène, pp. 28, 29, 35; National Archives of Canada, pp. 30 [C-011016], 34 [C-9778], 42 (top [C-30811]), 42 (bottom [PA-112912]); Historic Urban Plans, Ithaca, New York, p. 31 (detail); Archive Photos, p. 33 (both); Port of Montreal Archives, pp. 40 [3211], 44 [325]; UPI/Corbis-Bettman, p. 43; Reuters/Corbis-Bettman, p. 71; © Winston Fraser, pp. 45, 56-57, 65 (top); © Robert Fried, pp. 46-47, 69 (left), 70 (bottom); Fednav, p. 50; Yves Marcoux/Tony Stone Images, p. 69 (right); © Benoit Chalifour, p. 72. Maps by Ortelius Design.

Copyright © 1997 by Lerner Publications Company

All rights reserved. International copyright secured. No part of this book may be reproduced, stored in a retrieval system, or transmitted in any form or by any means—electronic, mechanical, photocopying, recording, or otherwise— without the prior written permission of Lerner Publications Company, except for the inclusion of brief quotations in an acknowledged review.

LIBRARY OF CONGRESS CATALOGING-IN-PUBLICATION DATA

Hamilton, Janice.
    Destination Montreal / by Janice Hamilton.
       p. cm. — (Port cities of North America)
    Includes index.
    Summary: Discusses the geography, history, economy, and daily life of the port city of Montreal.
    ISBN 0–8225–2788–X (lib. bdg. : alk. paper)
    1. Montréal (Québec)—Juvenile literature. [1. Montréal (Québec)] I. Title. II. Series
F1054.5.M84H36 1997
971.4'27–dc20   96–38694

Manufactured in the United States of America
1 2 3 4 5 6 – JR – 02 01 00 99 98 97

The glossary that begins on page 76 gives definitions of words shown in **bold type** in the text.

CONTENTS

CHAPTER ONE	The Port on the River	7
CHAPTER TWO	From Canoes to Containers	27
CHAPTER THREE	The Global Connection	49
CHAPTER FOUR	The River and the Mountain	63
	Glossary	76
	Pronunciation Guide	77
	Index	78
	About the Author	80

CHAPTER ONE

THE PORT ON THE RIVER

The sun sets on downtown Montreal (facing page) *while the St. Lawrence River, integral to Montreal's economy, flows steadily in the background.*

Location ▶ The Port of Montreal lies on the St. Lawrence River 1,000 miles from the Atlantic Ocean. Even though it is so far inland, Montreal is one of the busiest seaports in North America. This is because Montreal is close to heavily populated cities and major manufacturing centers in the Canadian provinces of Ontario and Quebec, as well as to cities in the northeastern and midwestern regions of the United States. Products shipped between these areas and other parts of the world pass through the port.

The St. Lawrence River is one of the world's largest navigable waterways. It drains a vast area of North America, including the Great Lakes (Lakes Ontario, Erie, Huron, Superior, and Michigan) and major waterways such as the Ottawa, Richelieu, and Saguenay Rivers. The St. Lawrence flows in a northeasterly direction from Lake Ontario toward the river's mouth at the Gulf of St. Lawrence, an arm of the Atlantic Ocean.

The Great Lakes-St. Lawrence Seaway System links the Atlantic Ocean with the interior of North America. The Port of Montreal, described as a gateway to the continent, is an important stop for ships.

Montreal is in Quebec, a province in eastern Canada where the majority of the population speaks French. To the west of Quebec lie the province of Ontario and the cold waters of James and Hudson Bays. Along Quebec's southern border are the U.S. states of New York, Vermont, New Hampshire, and Maine, as well as the Canadian province of New Brunswick. The

Wharves parallel the river to provide ease in docking.

▶ Just upstream from the Port of Montreal are the Lachine Rapids, a 2.5-mile stretch of turbulent currents, shallow pools, and wooded islands. More than 50 species of fish live in the rapids' cold water, providing abundant food for ducks, gulls, and herons.

▶ Lake Ontario is 223 feet higher than the St. Lawrence River at Montreal. To move safely between the elevations of the river and the lake, a ship enters a gated lock in the St. Lawrence Seaway canal. The gates close, and the lock is either filled or emptied until the water reaches the same level as the next part of the canal. Ships pass through seven locks in the stretch of the Seaway lying between Montreal and Lake Ontario.

Gulf of St. Lawrence laps against Quebec's southeastern shores. The province of Newfoundland and Labrador borders Quebec to the east. Across Ungava Bay and Hudson Strait to the north is the new Canadian territory of Nunavut.

The port and the city are on the Island of Montreal. The island is shaped like a boomerang, with the port on the eastern outside curve. The outstanding feature of the island's otherwise flat terrain is the rounded summit of Mount Royal, an ancient volcano in the heart of the city.

The port extends 15 miles along the north shore of the St. Lawrence, from the eastern part of the island to the city's downtown core. A few piers sit at a right angle to the shore, but most wharves parallel the river. The wharves extend far past the original shoreline, which has been filled in with rocks and earth, enclosed with high cement walls at water's edge, and paved. The additional space increases storage capacity and puts the wharves in deep water.

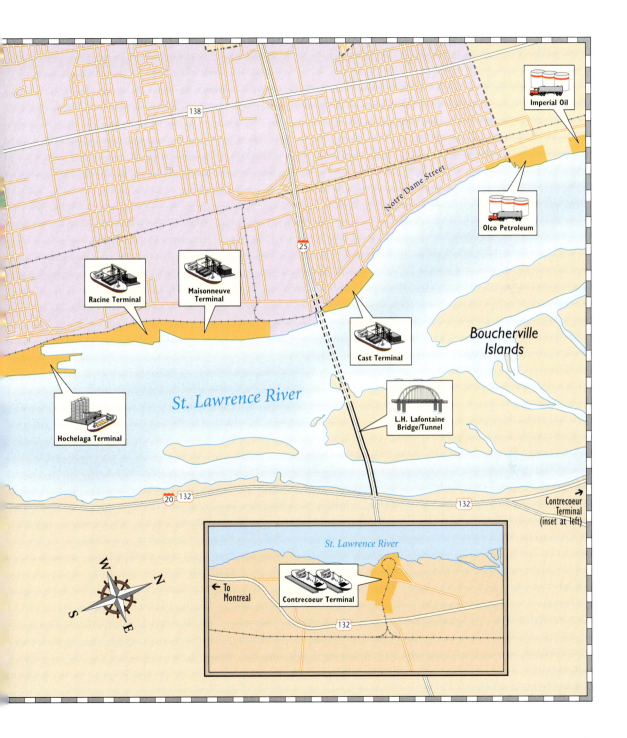

Railroad tracks run parallel to the docks. Just beyond the fenced-in yards and sheds where cargo is stored lies Notre Dame Street. This wide thoroughfare provides easy access to the city and to bridges leading off the island.

The Port of Montreal competes with other large ports on the eastern seaboard of North America. To attract business, these ports strive to keep their fees as low as possible. These fees include charges for services such as the use of wharves and rail facilities, as well as passenger charges and grain handling fees. The ports also work hard to offer safe, reliable, and efficient service to keep shippers coming back year after year.

The Port of Montreal handles a wide variety of ◀ **Cargo** trade products including nuts, vegetables, wine and other alcoholic beverages, lumber, chemical products, asbestos, steel, machinery, car parts, iron ore, scrap metal, coal, fertilizers, grain, and petroleum products. Montreal's

The many rail lines that service the port distribute containerized cargo from Montreal—Canada's number one container port—to destinations in Canada and the United States.

Thirteen computerized gantry cranes aid in loading and unloading the many container ships that call on the port. The cranes can unload a ship's cargo directly onto an awaiting truck.

specialty is containerized cargo. An endless variety of products arrives at the port by truck and rail in huge steel containers, which are then loaded onto oceangoing ships for export, or sale to other countries. Containers that are imported, or brought into the country from abroad, are then hauled by train or truck to their final destinations. The port's huge dockside **gantry cranes** load and unload containers quickly to and from ships.

Vessels from 15 different container shipping lines call at the Port of Montreal on a regular basis. Montreal is a terminus, or end point, for these lines, whose ships are completely unloaded and reloaded at the port. They may make more than one stop overseas to pick up or drop off additional containers.

*Two workers help maneuver a heavy block of stone, an example of the non-containerized **breakbulk cargo** handled by the port.*

About 50 percent of the container traffic in Montreal goes to or is sent from Canada, while the other half is bound for or comes from the United States. U.S. shippers like the Port of Montreal for several reasons. First, it is so far inland that very little of the journey to market is by overland transportation, which is more expensive than maritime transportation. Most of the expense is for shipping on water—the least

Pipes snake from trucks to a ship's cargo holds to transfer liquid cargo.

costly mode of commercial transportation. Also, part of the cost of transportation is in Canadian dollars, which are worth less than U.S. dollars. For this reason, U.S. shippers pay less for the journey to market.

In addition to serving container traffic, the Port of Montreal has facilities to handle loose, dry **bulk cargo,** such as salt and raw sugar, and pipelines for liquid bulk products, such as wine and fuel oil. The port also handles a wide variety of **general cargo,** or containerized and non-containerized items that are not shipped in bulk. General cargo includes food products, clothing, forest products, automobile parts, and other cargoes that are packaged in wooden cases, barrels, bags, or pallets. General cargo also includes huge pieces of heavy machinery that are too big to package or ship in a container. Non-containerized general cargo is sometimes referred to as breakbulk cargo.

Coming into Port ▶ Imagine you are on board a ship sailing to Montreal from Europe. At Les Escoumins, a Quebec town on the Lower St. Lawrence River, your ship takes on a pilot who is familiar with the river's currents and channels. A new pilot comes aboard at Quebec City, and pilots change again at Trois-Rivières, Quebec, about 80 miles downstream from Montreal.

To help your ship stay in the shipping channel between Quebec City and Montreal, red and green buoys and lighted beacons mark the way. Some ships also take advantage of an electronic navigation system. A satellite keeps track of each vessel's position and sends this information to the ship's onboard computer. The pilot or captain can view the ship, the buoys, and the shoreline, which are all charted on an electronic screen. This system helps ships navigate more safely through fog and darkness.

A series of electronic gauges in the water measures the depth at 13 sites along the channel and transmits the information to ships by computer. The average water level is about 38 feet. During a dry summer, the water level may reach only the minimum of 36 feet. Heavily laden ships need at least that much water to avoid running aground.

As your vessel approaches Montreal, the first port facilities to come into view are the oil-storage tanks at the eastern end of the Island of Montreal. Tankers carrying gasoline and other petroleum products dock here. The tankers are then hooked up to pipelines that transfer the liquid petroleum to storage tanks off the port property. Eight petroleum companies have wharves and storage facilities in Montreal, and the port can handle up to 14 tankers at a time.

In this section of the port, the 800-foot wide shipping channel hugs the north shore of the river. In the middle of the river, yellow buoys mark anchorage sites where ships can anchor if they have to wait for a berth, or parking spot, beside the dock.

After passing the petroleum section of the port, you will see the Cast Terminal, where huge dockside cranes tower over a ship, loading or unloading containers. Nearby a pair of towers, one on each shore, marks the presence of a tunnel built for car and truck traffic under the river. These towers circulate air underground. Power transmission lines span the

> ▶ Ships approaching Montreal's Old Port pass under the Jacques Cartier Bridge. The bridge, one of several that cross the St. Lawrence River, is a little over two miles long and has five lanes of traffic. At its highest point, the bridge towers 35 stories over the river.
>
> ▶ The Montreal Port Corporation has made a profit every year since 1979. In the 12-year period from 1984 through 1995, the port earned about 148 million Canadian dollars (U.S. $110 million).
>
> ▶ The Port of Montreal is Canada's number one container port.

The St. Lambert Lock (below) *is the first of a series of locks that incoming ships must pass through when they enter the St. Lawrence Seaway at Montreal. Some of the vessels that call on the Port of Montreal are oil tankers, which transfer their cargo through pipelines* (right) *to nearby oil storage tanks.*

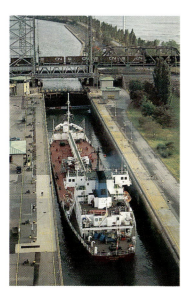

river. Another building, shaped something like an air-traffic control tower, houses Canadian Coast Guard radar equipment that monitors the movement of ships.

On the river's south shore, you may also see a marina for powerboats and sailboats. There is plenty of room on the river for pleasure boats as well as large ships, but to be on the safe side, small craft are supposed to stay in a special channel.

Just upstream from the marina is the mouth of the St. Lawrence Seaway. The Seaway, which extends from the eastern end of Lake Erie to Montreal, is a series of **locks** and canals that provides shipping access to the Great Lakes. The Great Lakes-St. Lawrence Seaway System allows oceangoing vessels to travel easily all the way from the Atlantic Ocean to the far western end of Lake Superior, a distance of 2,342 miles.

A YEAR-ROUND PORT

Every now and then, Port of Montreal staff have to answer a familiar question—is it really true that Montreal is open for business year-round? Given that the air temperature is generally at or below the freezing point from November through April, this skepticism is understandable. But the St. Lawrence River is navigable all year, at least for ships with hulls strengthened to withstand ice.

The river is kept open because the ice must be broken up to lower the risk of ice jams and floods that could damage riverside communities. At the same time, keeping the river ice-free allows commercial vessels to sail upstream to Montreal year-round.

The Canadian Coast Guard is responsible for keeping the navigational channel open. It has several **icebreakers** stationed on the river, including an icebreaker hovercraft. With their strong hulls and powerful engines, these vessels clear paths through the ice.

Icebreakers are only part of the story. The Coast Guard uses a variety of techniques to keep the channel clear. In late fall, log-shaped steel booms are placed along sections of the channel. The booms allow for a faster formation of a protective barrier of solid ice outside the shipping channel at Lake St. Pierre and other strategic locations. In forcing solid ice to form along the riverbanks rather than in the channel, the booms prevent loose ice from forming and help strengthen the water's current. The fast-moving water is then able to quickly evacuate any ice that makes its way into the channel.

The Coast Guard installs video cameras in known trouble spots to make sure ice doesn't block the channel. The Coast Guard also installs special winter buoys that can't be easily broken by the crushing pressure of the ice. The Coast Guard's responsibilities end at the port boundary. Within the port, the natural speed of the current, as well as the regular passage of ships, is enough to keep the channel clear.

The Canadian Coast Guard relies on different types of vessels to navigate the St. Lawrence River in the winter. Hovercrafts (right) *maneuver easily across the ice, while icebreakers* (below) *plow through the ice to keep the channel open for commercial shipping.*

Opposite the entrance to the Seaway is Île Sainte-Hélène (St. Helen's Island), the site of a large city park. Between this island and the Island of Montreal is a channel known as St. Mary's Current. Here the current increases speed to 4.5 knots an hour, compared with 2 knots an hour in wider sections of the river farther downstream.

A clock tower marks the entrance to the Old Port, where sturdy red tugboats are tied up when they aren't guiding ships to their berths. This is the site of the city's original port and settlement.

A cruise ship picks up passengers at the Iberville Passenger Terminal (above).

The Old Port clock tower (left) *welcomes shippers to the heart of the Port of Montreal.*

The shipping channel ends here, protected by a point of land called Cité du Havre, where the port administration building is located. You'll also see a container and general cargo terminal, and a massive, former grain elevator.

You may also note dock space for several harbor tour boats and passenger facilities for the many cruise ships that visit Montreal every year. Montreal is a popular tourist destination. Each year approximately 30,000 people pass through Iberville Passenger Terminal. In summer and in the fall, when the leaves turn red and gold, many travelers combine a visit to the city with a cruise on the beautiful St. Lawrence River.

Port Services ▶ The port is like a city within a city. It has its own railway, roads, electrical substations, water system, and security. While in port, ships may obtain food and other fresh provisions, fuel and diesel oil, and repairs. Crew members may be treated at several city hospitals.

The port provides visiting ships with basic services, including drinking water and electricity. Specialized facilities include a temperature-controlled warehouse for storing food items and a floating crane that can be moved wherever it is needed to lift extremely heavy cargo items. Some docks are equipped with ramps so trucks and trailers can drive directly onto and off of ships. When the Canadian Forces send peacekeepers to troubled spots overseas, they load tanks and trucks here.

Private companies provide shipping lines with river pilots and towing services. Not all ships need towing to a berth—it depends on

Three tugboats guide a giant tanker to its berth. Oceangoing ships have a distinctive bulbous bow to help them penetrate large ocean waves.

the size of the vessel, the location of the berth, and the speed of the current. Large vessels often need help maneuvering to their berths, especially if they have to squeeze into a spot between two other ships or beside a pier in the crowded Old Port.

◀ **Port Administration**

The Port of Montreal is run by the Montreal Port Corporation, a company owned by the Canadian government. The Port Corporation owns the land within the port territory and builds and repairs facilities, such as wharves and storage sheds, and rents them to stevedoring companies (which provide workers for loading and unloading ships). The corporation also operates a passenger terminal, a railway network, and a grain elevator.

This tall, gray, windowless building where grain is stored sticks out into the river at a slight angle. It has one berth for unloading grain-filled vessels from the Great Lakes region and two berths where vessels are loaded with grain for export. The elevator can store up to 286,596 tons of grain. Vessels can be unloaded at a rate of 3,307 tons per hour, while the automatic

A bulk carrier is loaded with grain for export.

loading facility can load a vessel with up to 4,960 tons of grain per hour.

More than 60 miles of railway tracks serve most berths, allowing easy access to the waterfront. The port's six busy locomotives can switch, or move around, up to 700 container railcars every day. The port's locomotives assemble container trains and take them to interchange areas, where locomotives belonging to CP Rail System or to CN North America (Canada's two major railway companies) pick them up.

A Visit to a Container Terminal

The port has five container terminals. One of them, Racine Terminal, is the busiest container terminal in Canada, handling about 250,000 containers a year. In front of the main Racine Terminal building, incoming trucks idle while their drivers go into the office. Terminal staff tell each driver exactly where to take the container for loading onto ships. Once the driver finds the right spot, a crane lifts the container off the back of the truck and stacks it with other containers waiting for the same ship.

Each container bears an identifying number. When an employee of a shipping line looks up that number in the company's computer, he or she can find out where the container is, what it is carrying, and what its destination is. Employees at the container terminal use the same shipping number to keep track of the container's location in the yard. But unlike shipping-line employees, terminal employees do not know what is inside a container. This policy is meant to discourage theft. All containers look the same and are securely sealed.

> ▶ Containers destined for the United States remain sealed and do not have to go through **customs** at the Port of Montreal. Some are pre-cleared aboard ship, while others clear customs after they cross the U.S. border.

Containers are sorted and stored in the yard so they can be easily loaded onto a ship without confusion. All containers for one vessel are kept together, sorted by port of destination and by weight, so that the heavier containers are loaded first at the bottom of the ship. Containers that need to be heated or refrigerated because they contain perishable products are plugged into special electrical outlets.

Precautions are taken for containers carrying hazardous products, which may be flammable, corrosive, or radioactive. Stickers with an internationally recognized code let terminal employees know which containers can be transported close together and which must be kept apart. For example, containers with radioactive contents should be kept away from the crew's living quarters on board ship. And, if a fire breaks out or a container is dropped, this code helps employees and firefighters handle the emergency.

When it is time to load a container onto a ship, a small flatbed truck gets the container from the yard. The driver takes it dockside and

From his perch, a gantry-crane operator (left) *watches an incoming ship. With his expert help, containers will be moved from ship to shore* (facing page) *as efficiently as possible.*

parks directly underneath a gantry crane. The crane's spreader, resembling a four-legged spider hanging from a cable, is lowered to pick up the container. Pins fit inside holes at each top and bottom corner to secure the container as it is moved through the air.

Two people work in the gantry crane. One, seated in a cab with a bird's-eye view of the yard and the vessel, is called the checker. This person has a list of which containers to load onto a particular ship. The checker is in contact by walkie-talkie with the yard truck drivers and the crane operator, who is perched in a second cab 110 feet above the ship's deck.

The crane operator uses electronic controls to move the spreader back and forth. He or she must judge by eye and by experience exactly when and where to lower the spreader. The system moves quickly and efficiently, and a minimum of 25 containers can be loaded each hour.

The process is reversed when a loaded ship arrives. About half the containers are unloaded and stacked in the yard to await pickup by truck. The others are taken to the rail sidings in the terminal and lifted onto flatbed railcars. Some containers go by rail to western Canada, but the three main rail destinations are Toronto, Detroit, and Chicago.

With its advanced technology, efficient transportation networks, and advantageous geographical location, it's no wonder the Port of Montreal is one of the busiest ports on the eastern seaboard of North America. Year-round, the port handles thousands of ships and millions of tons of cargo quickly and efficiently. Montreal is proud to be a major world port.

CHAPTER TWO

FROM CANOES TO CONTAINERS

John Young (facing page) *held various trade-related positions in Montreal in the mid-1800s. He was integral in ushering the port into an age of successful commerce.*

Hanging in the lobby of the Port of Montreal administration building is a portrait of a stern-looking, bearded gentleman named John Young. He is described as the "Father of the Port of Montreal" because in the mid-1800s he was responsible for launching port improvements, such as building wharves and deepening the St. Lawrence River channel. But the port's story began well before Young came on the scene.

Early Peoples ▶ Between 6,000 and 7,000 years ago, nomadic Native peoples settled in the St. Lawrence River valley. They made tools with chipped and ground

Iroquois Indians planted gardens to supply their communities with fresh vegetables to eat.

stone and lived by hunting game, fishing, and gathering berries. Over time the Native peoples learned to make pottery and, later, to farm.

Iroquois peoples, who may have descended from these early groups, were living in what is now the Montreal area when European explorers first arrived in the region in the 1500s. The Iroquois traveled on foot and by canoe, ate fish, game, and berries, and grew corn, beans, and squash.

French Explorers

French explorer Jacques Cartier was the first European to chart the St. Lawrence River and to visit what is now Montreal. In 1535 he traveled up the river as far as the Huron village of Hochelaga (modern-day Montreal). Like other

➤ Archaeologists have found bits of pottery, chipped stone flakes, and the remains of campfires in Old Montreal. This evidence shows that Native peoples used this area, perhaps for fishing, between A.D. 570 and 1510.

➤ Jacques Cartier's ship got stuck in shallow Lake St. Pierre, so he completed his journey to the Island of Montreal in two longboats. When Samuel de Champlain later visited the region, he came prepared with parts to build a small, lightweight sailing vessel at Tadoussac, on the Lower St. Lawrence, to complete the voyage up the river.

explorers of the time, Cartier was looking for a quick route from Europe to the markets of the Far East. In exploring North America, he and his crew hoped to find a water route across the continent. They also hoped to discover gold.

In his three trips to the St. Lawrence River valley, Cartier found neither gold nor a transcontinental water route. However, he did claim the land for the king of France. This claim eventually allowed the French to occupy and settle the interior of North America.

In the early 1600s, another French explorer, Samuel de Champlain, visited the St. Lawrence River valley. With help from the French government, Champlain hoped to build a settlement on the river so that France could take

Jacques Cartier was the first European to explore what would become Montreal.

advantage of the North American fur trade. Beaver and other furs were very popular for making hats and other fashionable clothes in Europe, and the best furs came from the northern forests of North America. Champlain began to make alliances with the Hurons and other regional Indian groups, who trapped fur-bearing animals for traders to ship back to Europe.

In 1608 Champlain built a fort and a warehouse 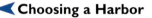 **Choosing a Harbor**
at the site of present-day Quebec City. This was the first permanent French settlement in North America, and Champlain became known as the "Father of New France." In 1611 Champlain sailed to the Island of Montreal and chose sites for a future harbor and settlement near the mouth of a small tributary, the St. Pierre River. Champlain chose well. Although the French

In 1611 Samuel de Champlain chose present-day Montreal as the site of a harbor and settlement in the French colony of New France.

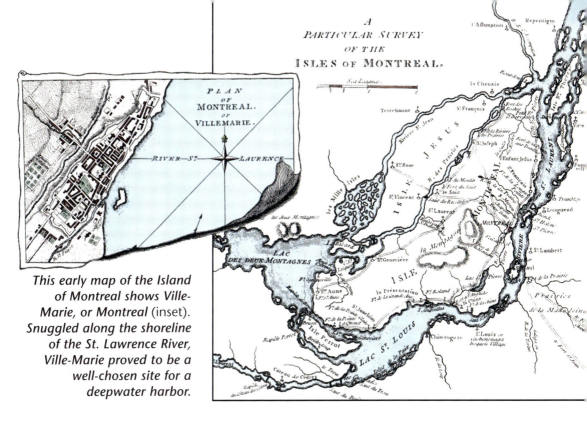

This early map of the Island of Montreal shows Ville-Marie, or Montreal (inset). Snuggled along the shoreline of the St. Lawrence River, Ville-Marie proved to be a well-chosen site for a deepwater harbor.

did not build an outpost immediately, the site he picked eventually became the little town of Ville-Marie, which grew into Montreal.

The spot he chose for the harbor was safe and sheltered from the fast-flowing current by a small island, Île Normandin (later known as Market Island). The water was deep enough for ships to anchor offshore, and there was a muddy, pebbly beach. The site was just below the Lachine Rapids, which blocked all ships from going any farther upstream.

The harbor site did have one drawback. The St. Mary's Current was so powerful that ships coming from Quebec City needed a very strong breeze behind them to get upstream. Ships sometimes took days to go just a few miles. Another problem was that Lake St. Pierre, about

60 miles downstream from Montreal, was too shallow for large oceangoing ships to navigate. Hundreds of years later, the port would turn out to have one major advantage—there was room to expand for many miles along the riverbank.

In 1642 Paul de Chomedey de Maisonneuve and about four dozen French colonists landed at the spot Champlain had chosen. Their main goal was to convert the Indian peoples of the region to Christianity. The mission had many difficulties, however. The French colonists had to move the settlement to higher ground because the river flooded the first winter. In addition, Iroquois groups often attacked the settlement, trying to gain control of the area's fur trade, from which the French had excluded them. As a result, the mission was not a great success. The settlement remained small for decades, with a population of just 1,000 people in 1700.

The Fur Trade and the Seven Years' War

Over time Montreal became a very successful fur-trading center, partly because it was so easy to reach. The island was near the junction of the St. Lawrence and the Ottawa Rivers—two major water routes to the North American interior. Every summer for more than a century, a huge fur fair was held near Montreal's waterfront. Indian trappers, some of whom had traveled 1,000 miles, arrived in one large flotilla of several hundred canoes. They traded the pelts of beavers, otters, mink, and moose to European traders for manufactured goods such as guns and ammunition, cloth, copper kettles, jewelry, and rum.

> ▶ Up to 45 feet long, bateaux could carry 1,500 pounds of freight. Durham boats, or barges with sails, also plied the waters between Quebec City and Montreal.

(Above) *Indians brought highly valued beaver pelts to French traders. By the 1700s, fur trading had become a booming business in North America. As trade grew in Montreal, water travel* (below) *was the most efficient means of getting from place to place.*

Part of New France until the mid-1700s, Montreal was the commercial and military center of the French colony, while Quebec City (an important port for oceangoing vessels) was the administrative capital. The Seven Years' War (1756-1763) in Europe, however, changed the destiny of New France. The British and the French carried their dispute to the shores of North America, and in 1759 British forces defeated the French at Quebec City. The next summer, the British surrounded Montreal and the town surrendered without a shot fired. Montreal became part of a British colony, known at first as the Province of Quebec, then as Lower Canada.

During the 1700s, water provided the primary method of transportation in this part of the world. But most oceangoing ships did not attempt to navigate the shallow waters of Lake St. Pierre. Instead the cargo was transferred at Quebec City to commercial riverboats, such as canoes and flat-bottomed boats called bateaux, for the trip upriver to Montreal.

In 1809 Montreal businessman John Molson built the first steamboat for the run between Quebec City and Montreal. By 1819 seven steamboats competed for business, impressing passengers with their comfort and prompt service—the steamboats made the trip between the two cities in only 36 hours.

The Port of Montreal in the 1800s

The steamer Canada *was one of the many steamships that helped usher in a new era of shipping and long-distance travel.*

Despite this improvement, the port at Montreal remained a primitive affair. Local residents threw garbage and waste along the riverbanks. The port had no wharves, so passengers walked on planks to reach the shore, and goods were unloaded onto the beach, whether muddy or dry.

By 1824 two rough wooden wharves had been built, and a few dirt roads descended directly to the edge of the water. Large items were pulled to shore with cables. Other developments cemented Montreal's role as an early hub of transportation. Workers completed the Lachine Canal in 1825 so that people and goods traveling by boat to what is now Ontario would

The Lachine Canal allowed ships to circumnavigate the dangerous Lachine Rapids.

> ▶ In 1830, 43,000 square yards of earth were brought from the Lachine Canal to be used as landfill for new docks at the port.

not have to disembark for the nine-mile journey by road around the Lachine Rapids. The entrance to the canal was built next to the harbor so small riverboats could tie up beside ocean-going vessels to transfer cargo. Meanwhile locks and canals were constructed to bypass other rapids on the Upper St. Lawrence River.

By 1830 local business and government leaders determined that additional improvements were still needed. Over the next few years, thousands of feet of new stone docks were built. Ramps for unloading cargo, a bridge to Market Island where the main wharf was located, and retainment walls to protect the riverbank from floods were built as well.

In 1851 a major obstacle to transportation on the St. Lawrence was overcome—a channel was dredged (dug) through Lake St. Pierre. The channel was deep enough to allow oceangoing vessels to reach the port at Montreal. Along with the enlargements and improvements to the Lachine Canal, the new channel boosted Montreal from a river port to an ocean port for the first time.

In the mid-1800s, Montreal's waterfront bustled with activity. Steamers and oceangoing ships, some of which were powered by a combination of steam and sail, plied the waters. Immigrants, manufactured goods, and mail arrived at the port from England and Scotland. Exports shipped through Montreal included grain, lumber, and potash. By 1871 Montreal's wharves extended nearly three miles to the east of the original harbor, and trains served the docks.

Massive timber rafts were another familiar sight on the St. Lawrence River. Lumberjacks in the forests of Ontario cut the timber. Squared logs were then tied together in rafts up to a quarter of a mile long. The rafts were floated to the head of the Lachine Rapids, where they were taken apart for the trip through the rocky rapids. The rafts were tied together again near the Montreal harbor, then floated to Quebec City to be loaded onto ships bound for England. There, the wood was sawed into lumber and used for building and carpentry. The last timber rafts came through Montreal in 1911. After that, timber was sawed into pieces of lumber in Canadian sawmills, sent by rail to the port at Quebec City, and then shipped overseas.

> ▶ Around 1840 (no one is sure exactly when), the Port of Montreal began awarding a top hat to the captain of the first oceangoing vessel to reach the city each year. Eventually the top hat was replaced by a cane with a gold tip.

In winter ice floes (below) *piled up on the city's riverbanks. In spring melting ice and snow flooded Montreal's streets. In 1886 floodwaters stopped trains dead in their tracks* (right).

Winter was one of the biggest challenges facing the Port of Montreal. Above Quebec City, the river would freeze solid, and ice generally would close the Port of Montreal for at least four months a year. In the Gulf of St. Lawrence, drifting **ice floes** made navigation impossible. The sight of the first ship of spring coming into port bringing fashions, food, and mail from Europe was always a cause for celebration.

Another problem plagued Montreal—floods. Although the Great Lakes acted as a giant reservoir, holding back some of the melted snow, the St. Lawrence River rose each spring. The most disastrous floods occurred when the ice piled up at various points and blocked the river. When an ice jam developed, the water would rise swiftly behind it, flooding homes and businesses on low land. Terrible floods occurred in Montreal in 1857, 1861, and 1886.

SIR HUGH ALLAN

The Port of Montreal helped put the city on the map in more ways than one. In the mid-1800s, Montreal became the capital of Canadian business and industry. One of the key people who made that happen started out in the shipping business.

Hugh Allan (1810-1882) was born in Scotland, where his father was in the shipping business. At age 13, he went to work in another family business, a counting house. At 16 he emigrated to Montreal, where he worked first for a grain merchant and later for a leading import company. When he was 25, Allan became part owner of that firm.

Allan's family in Scotland loaned the import company money to buy several ships, including oceangoing vessels and a steamer for the Quebec City-Montreal run. It became the largest shipping company in Montreal and was known as the Allan Line. Allan's ocean steamers used the latest technologies, such as screw propellers and iron hulls.

In 1856, with the support of some of Allan's political friends, his company got a government contract to provide regular mail service between England, Montreal, and Portland, Maine. The ships carried not only mail, but also troops, immigrants, and general cargo.

Allan expanded into other businesses in the 1860s and 1870s. He participated in insurance companies, started a bank, and was president of a telegraph company. His investments in mining, especially coal, fueled railways, steamships, and factories. He also organized financing for new manufacturing industries such as textiles, steel, tobacco, paper, and shoemaking. These companies provided jobs for the immigrants who came to Canada on Allan Line ships.

The working conditions in Allan's factories were poor, and he was criticized for trying to influence politicians. However, many people considered Allan a model citizen, and he was given the title Sir Hugh Allan by Queen Victoria in 1871.

A portrait of Sir Hugh Allan (right) *reveals the shipping magnate's powerful stature. In the early 1900s, immigrants from Europe arrived at the Allan Line docks* (below), *where many of them found jobs.*

Port improvements continued into the early 1900s. In 1901 a high stone wall was built to protect the harbor area from floods. The channel was dredged to a depth of 30 feet and the old wharves were replaced by high piers in deeper water. By 1909 there were steel storage sheds, paved roads, and grain elevators. Canadian Vickers, a privately owned company, opened a yard for ship construction and repairs in 1912. The port also was made safer with the organization of the harbor police department in 1913. Rail lines were extended along the docks, and by 1914, the port had 40 miles of tracks. And in 1917, the Imperial Oil wharf was completed to handle imported oil.

During World War I (1914-1918), the military guarded the port. No one could enter without a special pass, and ship arrival and departure times were kept secret to prevent enemy attacks. After the war, commercial business rebounded,

◀ **The Port of Montreal in the 1900s**

The Port of Montreal's first police forces patrolled the area on motorcycle.

Dockworkers manually load sacks of grain from a Canadian Pacific freight car into a ship's cargo holds for export in the early 1900s. By the 1920s, grain elevators and grain-loading conveyor systems allowed large quantities of grain to enter and leave the port.

and a locomotive shop at the harbor yard and a cold storage warehouse were built.

In the early 1900s, the majority of exports from the port were destined for England, Canada's major trading partner, and other European countries. Canada had a wealth of natural resources, and the bulk of exports were raw materials and agricultural products such as grains and live cattle. Industrial exports included automobile parts, pulp and paper products, copper, and agricultural tools. Sugar and other raw materials that couldn't be grown in Canada's climate were imported through the Port of Montreal.

By 1928 three grain-storage elevators towered over the waterfront, and Montreal was known as the greatest grain harbor in the world. In that year, 95 million bushels of Canadian wheat, 76 million bushels of American wheat, and 356,000 tons of flour were exported from the Port of Montreal.

Traffic at the Port of Montreal slowed during the Great Depression of the 1930s. During this global economic downturn, 40 percent of working people in Montreal lost their jobs. About half as many tons of goods passed through the Port of Montreal as in the late 1920s. Exports of Canadian and U.S. grain dropped dramatically as well, partly due to the growth of competing ports in Canada and in the United States.

Quebec's economy improved during World War II (1939-1945). Montreal industries produced tanks, planes, and ships for the war effort. The port handled tons of coal, steel, iron, and other materials that were shipped to the city to help meet wartime industrial demand.

The St. Lawrence Seaway

For many years, people had talked about the need to deepen and otherwise improve the locks and canals linking the St. Lawrence River

The Great Depression hit Montreal hard, and some families who couldn't afford their rent were evicted from their homes (above). *But the economy came back during World War II. Since many men were shipped overseas to fight, women gained employment in factories* (left) *supplying the war effort.*

The completion of the St. Lawrence Seaway (1959) opened new horizons for shipping in North America. U.S. president Eisenhower and Great Britain's Queen Elizabeth II (both onboard) were among the first passengers to sail the newly opened Seaway.

▶ Building the section of the St. Lawrence Seaway between Montreal and Lake Ontario was a massive project. A large section of land was flooded. Roads, houses, and 6,500 people had to be moved to two newly created towns.

to the Great Lakes so that large oceangoing vessels could reach the markets of the Great Lakes region. Construction of the St. Lawrence Seaway started in 1954, despite the objections of Montrealers who worried that their port would lose business if ocean ships could sail farther inland. The Seaway opened in 1959 and is used mainly by bulk carriers that carry raw materials from other countries and ports on the Lower St. Lawrence River to industries on the Great Lakes.

The Seaway did not bring about the disaster some had anticipated for Montreal. Since the completion of the Seaway, shippers have begun using larger, more efficient vessels. The Seaway is not deep enough or wide enough to handle many of these ships, and enlarging the locks yet again would be too expensive. Furthermore, ice closes the Seaway between the end of December and the beginning of April.

In 1962 the Canadian Coast Guard began using icebreakers and ice-control booms on the St. Lawrence River to keep a channel open in winter. The main goal of breaking up the ice was to protect river communities from flooding. But it also made winter navigation possible. On January 4, 1964, a Danish merchant ship, the *Helga Dan,* became the first ship to reach Montreal during the first month of the calendar year. With the ship's arrival, Montreal officially became a year-round port. The port's manager presented the captain with a gold-headed cane, a tradition dating to the mid-1800s.

Over time many of the industries that had sprung up close to Montreal's waterfront in the 1800s closed. As good roads and highways were built around Montreal, industries no longer had to be next door to the port. As a result, many manufacturing companies were able to move to locations farther from the port when they chose to expand or modernize their facilities.

◀ **Winter Challenges**

▶ In 1968 Montreal's first container terminal opened for business.

Guy Beaudet (center) *of the Port of Montreal presented Captain Hindberg* (left) *of the* Helga Dan *with a gold-headed cane for being the earliest arrival to the Port of Montreal in 1964.*

The original, bustling site of the Port of Montreal has become the Old Port—a recreation area where visitors can tour museums or just sit in the park. Over the years, the port has expanded farther downstream.

The heart of the working port also moved from the Old Port to areas downstream because expanded storage space for container terminals and other modern port facilities were available in these areas. Although the Old Port could have been abandoned, the Canadian government saw other possibilities. In 1981 the government set up a corporation to develop the Old Port area as a park. The project was completed in 1992. A grain elevator that blocked the view of the river was torn down so people could see the water. Old waterfront sheds now house science exhibits, a flea market, and a movie theater. A housing development project will also bring new life to the area.

The Future of the Port ▶ Montreal is a successful port, but there are questions about its future. One question arises from Quebec's political situation. Many Quebecers want the province to separate from

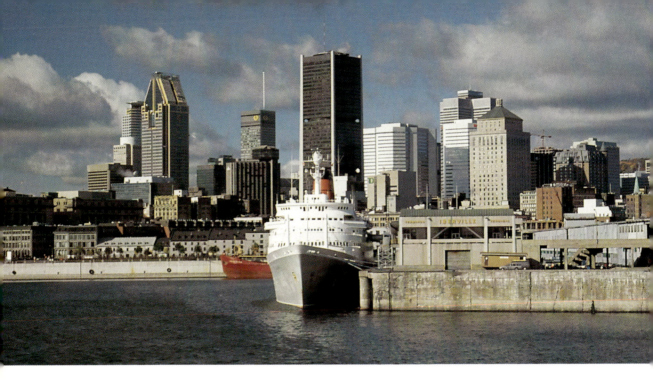

New horizons await the Port of Montreal.

Canada and become an independent nation. The move for independence has not had an immediate, direct impact on the port, but the political uncertainty has affected the economy of Montreal. Some companies don't want to invest in an area they view as politically unstable, and a number of companies have moved their head offices and plants to other cities. If Quebec does separate from Canada, some foreign shippers might also worry about the area's political instability.

Another problem is that the port could eventually run out of space for expansion on the Island of Montreal. Container terminals require large expanses of land for sorting and storing containers. Much of the port's land is crowded between the St. Lawrence River, the railway tracks, and Notre Dame Street. In 1988 the port assembled a property of about 740 acres in

Contrecoeur, Quebec, a small riverside community about 25 miles downstream from Montreal, so that future container operations can expand. The access from the river is good, and a highway and CN rail tracks serve the area. However, critics say expanding port operations off the Island of Montreal will take business out of the city and harm its economy. Others argue that the expansion is necessary for the port's continued growth and will help the city's economy.

To remain a vital international port, Montreal must continue to serve the large markets of Ontario and of the northeastern and midwestern regions of the United States. Otherwise, the port will become simply a regional facility. Factors beyond the port's control—rail shipping rates, fees at competing ports, the value of the Canadian dollar, and the desire and ability of nations to engage in trade—will all come into play.

The Port of Montreal has been intimately connected with the city since the first European missionaries set up their small settlement there. The port is key to Montreal's role as a transportation center and is a small gem in the city's economy. Port officials are optimistic about the port's future. Well situated geographically, the port offers competitive fees and is working hard to continue to attract business from Ontario and the United States. Montreal is also handling record amounts of containerized cargo each year. Forecasts suggest that containerized traffic will continue to grow into the next century, helping to ensure Montreal's place as a world-class port.

CHAPTER THREE

THE GLOBAL CONNECTION

The Port of Montreal is linked to more than 200 ports worldwide. A variety of ores (facing page) *are imported from as nearby as the United States and as far away as South Africa.*

Trade, or the exchange of goods and services, is the engine that runs the world's economy. Trade is especially important for Canada, which exports more than 165 billion Canadian dollars (U.S. $123 billion) of goods and services a year. The incomes of at least 3 million Canadians, from dockworkers to factory employees, depend directly on international trade.

Canada exports a greater proportion of what it produces than any other major industrial country. In the mid-1990s, more than 36 percent of all the goods and services Canadians produced were sold abroad. Total exports of

Road equipment and hardware are just some of the cargoes shipped to the island province of Newfoundland through the Port of Montreal.

goods increased by 56 percent, and imports grew by 48 percent.

About three-quarters of Canada's international trade is with the United States. This trade does not really affect the Port of Montreal, however, because most traffic between Canada and the United States goes by rail or truck.

Trading Partners

The growing importance of world trade has meant booming business for the Port of Montreal. Total traffic at the port was more than 21 million tons per year in the mid-1990s, and port administrators expect future increases, especially in international containerized cargo.

About 70 percent of trade through the Port of Montreal is international. The remaining 30 percent is domestic. Domestic trade refers to goods bought and sold within a country. Food, medicine, and other supplies sent to the Canadian Arctic during the ice-free summer months are examples of domestic trade going through the Port of Montreal. Another example is the twice-weekly service to the island province of Newfoundland. Household goods, building supplies, and other products are shipped to the province, while paper products are transported from Newfoundland.

Montreal is linked by almost 40 shipping lines to more than 200 ports on five continents. The port at Montreal serves as a main gateway for Canadian (and some American) trade with Europe, South America, Africa, and the Caribbean. One of the keys to Montreal's success is geography—the St. Lawrence River leads to the shortest route across the Atlantic Ocean, linking the markets of eastern Canada and the midwestern and northeastern United States to the markets of northern Europe and the Mediterranean region.

This North Atlantic trade route is one of the busiest in the world. Some 70 percent of Montreal's general cargo goes to and comes from trading partners in the United Kingdom and northern Europe. Another 20 percent goes to and from Mediterranean countries. Among the major ports with regular shipping connections to Montreal are Liverpool, Felixstowe, and London Thamesport in the United Kingdom, Le Havre and Fos in France, Antwerp and Zeebrugge in Belgium, Lisbon in Portugal, Cádiz and Valencia in Spain, Livorno, Genoa, and Naples in Italy, St. Petersburg in Russia, and Hamburg and Bremerhaven in Germany.

A ship and tugboats dock in the Port of Hamburg, Germany—one of the many international links to the Port of Montreal.

The Canmar Courage, *completed in 1996, can carry 2,200 TEUs (20-foot equivalent units). The vessel is 708 feet long by 106 feet wide and was specially designed to travel the St. Lawrence River.*

◀ **Containerized Cargo**

The Port of Montreal is Canada's number one container port. In the mid-1990s, a record 7.8 million tons of containerized imports and exports passed through the port each year. Containers carry almost any product imaginable, including meat products, sunflower seeds, waste and scrap paper, glass, electrical equipment, and fertilizers.

Fifteen container shipping lines involved in international trade regularly serve Montreal. Many call there weekly, while others call once every 10 days or monthly. Some of the ships that visit Montreal can each carry more than 2,000 **TEUs** (20-foot equivalent units) of containers.

One of the major advantages of containers is that they can be transferred rapidly from a ship to the back of a truck or to a flat railcar. This method of shipping goods, involving several modes (types) of transportation, is called **intermodal transportation.**

▶ Container traffic is usually expressed in 20-foot equivalent units, or TEUs. A container that is 20 feet long, by 8 feet wide, by 8.5 feet or 9.5 feet high is one TEU. A container that is 40 feet long, or double the size of a regular container, is described as two TEUs.

> ➤ In 1995 the Port of Montreal handled 352,022 TEUs inbound, weighing 3.6 million tons. Outbound container traffic came to 374,413 TEUs, weighing 4.2 million tons.
>
> ➤ Montreal's container terminals sometimes play an unwanted role in criminal activities. Some of the cars stolen in the city are hidden in containers and shipped abroad for sale. Illegal drugs occasionally slip into the country the same way.

About 40 percent of the containerized imports and exports passing through the port are transported by truck. Montreal is less than a day's drive to large cities such as Toronto, Quebec City, Boston, and Buffalo (New York). Sixty percent of containerized traffic moves by rail. By train, a container can be in Toronto 10 hours after it lands in Montreal or reach Detroit in 25 hours. Total time to Chicago is about 35 hours. In 1984 that connection took 72 hours. But railway companies, terminal operators, and shipping lines worked together—by reducing the number of times railcars had to be switched at the port, for example—to cut transportation time.

The fact that the Port of Montreal serves a vast, heavily populated area of North America also benefits shippers. Larger volumes of goods pass through the port than if it simply served the Montreal region. With larger volumes of cargo, shippers are able to keep costs down and to offer their customers more frequent service and a greater choice of international ports of call.

General Cargo ➤ Montreal handles large quantities of non-containerized general cargo, or breakbulk cargo. Breakbulk cargo can range from granite blocks or pieces of machinery too big to fit in containers, to boxes of oranges from South Africa and bags of cocoa beans from Nigeria and Ghana. The port is trying to increase business by attracting more non-containerized general cargo. A cargo-handling center, where most breakbulk-handling equipment and specially trained dockworkers would be in one place, is in the planning stages.

FROM FOREST TO FURNITURE

Baillie Lumber Company, a hardwood lumber company based in New York, sells 150 million board feet (354,000 cubic meters) of lumber every year to customers all over the world. It ships red and white oak, maple, ash, and cherry wood to Europe, the Middle East, and South Africa via the Port of Montreal.

The wood is cut in forests throughout New York and Pennsylvania and is then taken to sawmills where it is cut, dried in kilns, sorted, and packaged for export. Baillie's shipping manager chooses between several methods of shipping the lumber, depending on which is cheapest and most efficient for that particular shipment. Sometimes the lumber is placed in a container at the plant and driven directly to the Port of Montreal. In other cases, the lumber is put on a flatbed truck and taken to a Montreal warehouse belonging to a freight forwarder or to a trucking company for storage. Then the lumber is put into a container at the warehouse or taken to the port as breakbulk cargo.

The shipping manager decides whether to send a shipment in containers or breakbulk, depending on the cost and availability of vessels and handling services. If the lumber is going to a European country with modern port facilities, it will probably be shipped in a container. Older ports in other parts of the world, however, may not have container service.

Once overseas the lumber may be warehoused by an importer until it is sold, or it may be delivered directly to a manufacturer. The manufacturer turns the rough lumber into a variety of products, such as door moldings, wooden flooring, kitchen cabinets, furniture, and guitars. These products eventually end up in stores where building contractors, homeowners, and other consumers can purchase them.

Traffic in imports and exports of breakbulk goods can vary dramatically from year to year, depending on a variety of factors, such as competition from other ports and the ability of consumers to buy trade goods. For example, one year in the mid-1990s saw large quantities of steel imported through Montreal. The next year, because the North American economy was weak, fewer people bought new cars. As a result, there was less demand for steel to make cars, and steel imports declined.

Dry Bulk Cargo ► Montreal is an entry point for dry bulk cargo. Eighty percent of these raw materials are imported from other countries to supply industries such as steelmakers and sugar refineries in the Montreal area. The main dry bulk products handled by the port are iron ore, salt, gypsum, raw sugar, manganese ore, and coal. In the mid-1990s, the port handled 4.4 million tons of dry bulk each year.

Phosphate rock, coal, and fertilizers are shipped to Montreal from the United States.

Cranes are equipped with clamshell scoops to transfer ore dockside from a parked freighter.

Manganese ore comes from South Africa, and raw sugar comes from South Africa, Cuba, and Mozambique. Coke (a fuel made from coal) arrives via the Seaway from Illinois and Ohio, and some of it is then exported to Spain. Every autumn, mountains of salt accumulate on the docks. The salt, which comes from Ohio and Ontario, is spread on Montreal's streets to break up ice and snow during winter.

As for dry bulk exports, scrap metal is sent to South Korea, Taiwan, Turkey, and the United States. Zinc ore is transported to Belgium, the Netherlands, Bulgaria, and Italy.

Other dry bulk products are examples of domestic trade. Iron ore comes from Port Cartier, on the north shore of the Lower St. Lawrence. Gypsum and coal come from Nova Scotia.

> ▶ Petroleum terminals at the Port of Montreal can handle 14 tankers at a time. Tankers transport gasoline, fuel oil, naphtha, and other petroleum products.
>
> ▶ The port's grain elevator can unload ships at the rate of 3,307 tons an hour. Loading goes even faster—4,960 tons per hour!

Grain is a very important dry bulk product. ◀ **Grain**
Montreal was one of the world's biggest grain ports for decades. In 1980 a record total of 8.2 million tons of waterborne grain traffic passed in and out of the port. Grain traffic patterns have changed, however. In the mid-1990s, the port handled only 1.9 million tons of grain traffic a year. Most of Canada's grain is now sold to countries in the Far East, rather than to Europe, so most of it is exported from ports on the Pacific coast instead. A small proportion of the grain that passes through the Port of Montreal is purchased by local flour mills.

Grain comes by train from the farms of Canada's Prairie Provinces (Alberta, Saskatchewan, and Manitoba) to Thunder Bay, Ontario, which lies on the western shore of Lake Superior. There the grain is loaded onto ships called lakers, designed specifically to carry bulk products on the Great Lakes. The lakers follow the Great Lakes-St. Lawrence Seaway System to Montreal. After discharging their grain, lakers usually go to Port Cartier or Sept-Îles on the Lower St. Lawrence to pick up iron ore or other minerals for the return trip. These products are destined for industries in the Great Lakes area.

Petroleum and Liquid Bulk Cargo ▶ Petroleum products shipped to the Port of Montreal are destined for the Montreal market. Heating fuel oil comes from Venezuela, Texas, the United Kingdom, and a refinery in Quebec City. Gasoline for cars comes from Quebec City, France, the Netherlands, and Puerto Rico. In the mid-1990s, about 5 million tons of petroleum products came through the port each year. But the amount varies considerably from year to year, depending on various factors. Consumers buy more heating fuel during cold winters, for example. The price of petroleum products compared with other energy sources also impacts the amount of petroleum people buy.

Besides petroleum, products shipped as bulk liquids include molasses, vegetable oils, wine, and chemicals. The port handles about 771,000 tons of liquid bulk products (apart from petroleum) each year.

Fields of golden wheat are ripe for the picking. Even with improved grain storage and handling facilities, the Port of Montreal ships much less grain than in previous years due to changing trade patterns, which favor ports on the Pacific coast.

Although more goods are exported through the Port of Montreal than are imported, the port has a fairly equal **balance of trade.** Shipping lines like to have an even balance because it is expensive for them to travel fully loaded one way and to return with empty holds.

◀ **Balance of Trade**

The balance of trade between two countries depends partly on the relative value of their money. For example, if the value of the German deutsche mark is higher than that of the Canadian dollar, people in Germany may find the prices of Canadian products attractive. In recent years, the value of currencies such as the deutsche mark, the Japanese yen, and the U.S. dollar have been higher than the Canadian dollar, so Canada's exports have been high.

Canada has a small population, and consumers have not had a lot of extra money to spend in recent years. For Canadian manufacturers, the high level of exports has meant increased sales and less dependence on the small Canadian market.

But to be successful, exporters must know what people in other countries need and want as well as what they are willing to pay for the goods. Additionally, exporters must be aware of limits, restrictions, and special duties (taxes) that other countries may place on certain imports. Many governments purposely impose tariffs (fees) on imports to make them more expensive. This practice, called protectionism, encourages consumers in the importing country to buy less expensive, locally made products instead. This, in turn, protects the jobs of the workers who make those products in the importing country.

Trade Agreements and Teamwork

Countries around the world are moving toward opening up trade. The World Trade Organization has a membership of 116 countries. These countries are slowly bringing tariffs down, and international trade is increasing.

In 1994 Canada, the United States, and Mexico signed the North American Free Trade Agreement (NAFTA). This agreement lowers or removes barriers to trade among these countries. NAFTA has not had much impact on the Port of Montreal, however, since most goods going between Canada and the rest of North America travel overland. Goods manufactured in Montreal and sold in New York City or Chicago, for example, might be packed in containers and transported by road or rail but not by water. NAFTA does not apply to goods passing through Montreal on their way between the United States and other trading nations.

By the year 2005, the free trade agreement may be expanded to include Central and South America. And by the year 2010, there may be a free trade area including countries rimming the Pacific Ocean.

Trade remains a complicated business. Small and medium-sized companies usually do not have the time or the expertise to deal with overseas markets. The Canadian government, like other governments, has programs to assist would-be exporters and importers with international business. Companies may also turn to trading houses for help. In fact, about a quarter of the trading houses in Canada are located in Montreal.

Trading houses handle more than 50 percent of Canadian exports to destinations outside the

United States. These houses act as intermediaries between Canadian manufacturers and foreign buyers of goods and services. They can identify potential markets abroad, find buyers, negotiate prices, make financial arrangements, and prepare export documents. They can also find people to distribute goods overseas and to help with advertising and promotion.

Freight forwarders help companies with the transportation aspect of importing and exporting. A freight forwarder acts like a travel agent for cargo, looking for the fastest and most economical steamship company to move a customer's shipment. There are dozens of freight forwarding companies in Montreal, with offices either close to the airports or in small office buildings in Old Montreal.

The Port of Montreal handles a variety of general cargo, including boxed oranges.

A number of professionals keep the port running smoothly, including dockworkers, computer technicians, crane operators, customs officers, and tugboat pilots.

A freight forwarder can help an importer in Canada arrange with a European manufacturer to transport a product to port and turn the package over to the steamship line for the trip to Montreal. When the package arrives in Montreal, the forwarder can act as a customs broker (doing paperwork and paying duties) and have the package delivered to the importer.

A freight forwarder can also arrange for goods to be put into containers. If an exporter doesn't have enough merchandise to fill a container, for example, the forwarder will consolidate shipments from several customers. The forwarder can also arrange for insurance to cover the trade goods in case a vessel sinks, dockworkers strike, war breaks out, or the overseas buyer refuses to pay. From importers to shipping lines, port employees to freight forwarders, international trade requires teamwork.

CHAPTER FOUR

THE RIVER AND THE MOUNTAIN

Street performers in Old Montreal (facing page) *play to an audience in Jacques Cartier Square.*

On warm weekends, the riverside park at the Old Port of Montreal is usually crowded. Cyclists whiz along the park's broad sidewalks, while families sit on the grass, enjoying ice-cream cones. Visitors stroll slowly along the waterfront and read the plaques that describe the area's history or listen to the musicians who have set themselves up at strategic spots, hoping people will toss them a few coins.

A Great Place to Live ▶ The Old Port is just one of many attractions that contribute to Montreal's ranking as one of the best cities in the world in which to live.

Notre Dame de Bon Secours Chapel is an example of the old architecture that lines the streets of Old Montreal. The chapel boasts an interior of beautiful woodwork and stained-glass windows.

Montreal is Canada's second largest urban center and the second largest French-speaking city in the world after Paris.

Facing the river and the waterfront park are the gray stone buildings of Old Montreal. A few of these commercial buildings are more than 250 years old. In this neighborhood are the magnificent Notre Dame Basilica, the Old St. Sulpice Seminary built in 1683, and City Hall, which overlooks the outdoor restaurants of Jacques Cartier Square.

The core of Montreal is laid out on broad steps that rise gently toward the steep upper slopes of Mount Royal. The modern high-rises

Tourists can take in the view of Montreal and the river from a lookout atop Mount Royal.

of the downtown business district sit a step above and slightly to the west of Old Montreal. Behind them is Mount Royal. The park at the top of the mountain is a popular spot for walking, for cross-country skiing in winter, and for enjoying the view from the lookout.

If you head underneath the downtown office towers, you'll find an 18-mile network of underground passages known as the Underground City. These tunnels connect shops, theaters, restaurants, and banks with office buildings, hotels, train stations, and the Metro—Montreal's fast, quiet subway system. The Underground City is particularly busy at lunchtime, when office workers go there to eat, chat with friends, or do errands.

Montreal's Underground City (below) is an amazing network of tunnels. People can commute to work, go shopping, or take in a show, all without going above ground.

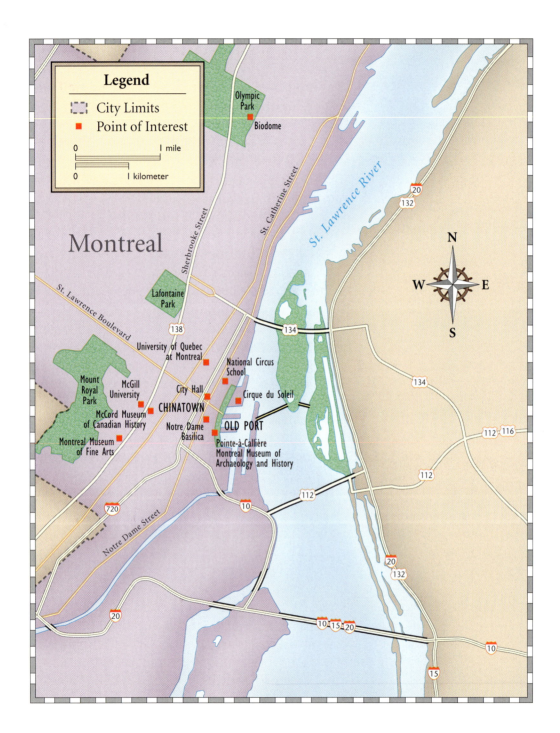

The Montreal region is well served by transportation facilities besides the port. There are two international airports as well as bus and rail services. Expressways and bridges crisscross the area.

Population and Ethnic Mix ▶ Many people who work in downtown Montreal live in residential suburbs on the Island of Montreal, in Laval (a separate municipality on a neighboring island to the north), or in communities on the south shore of the St. Lawrence. The total metropolitan area population is about 3 million people.

Municipalities on the Island of Montreal are joined in a regional organization called the Montreal Urban Community, or MUC, which is responsible for services such as police and bus service. The MUC, which includes the city of Montreal and 28 smaller municipalities, covers 193 square miles and has a population of about 1.8 million people.

The province of Quebec is the main center of North America's Francophone, or French-speaking, community. French is the official language of Quebec, and some 82 percent of the province's population learn French as a first language. In the Montreal region, 72 percent of the population have French as their first language, while 16 percent learn English first. Most members of the province's English community and other ethnic communities are located in or near Montreal. More than 60 percent of Montrealers are bilingual and can speak both English and French. Many Montrealers are multilingual, speaking three or more languages.

Lying on the outskirts of Montreal are two Mohawk Indian communities. Large Greek, Italian, Irish, and Jewish communities have also been established in the city for many years. More recent newcomers from Vietnam, Haiti, South and Central America, and the Middle East have settled in Montreal as well. They are encouraged to join in the French life of Montreal and, by law, must send their children to French schools.

The law in Quebec states that French is the official language of the provincial government, in the workplace, and on commercial and street signs. But consumer services—in stores and hospitals, for example—are frequently available in both English and in French. Montrealers can choose among a wide range of French and English radio and TV stations, as well as four daily newspapers, one in English and three in French. There are also English schools and theaters.

Since the end of the 1970s, Montreal's English community has been in decline. Some people have left because they did not like the language laws or the idea that the province might separate from Canada. Others simply found jobs in other parts of Canada. Most of the English people who still live in Montreal want their children to be bilingual and send them to French immersion schools, where much of the day is spent studying in French.

◀ Arts and Entertainment

The city's energetic arts community includes the Grands Ballets Canadiens dance company, the Montreal Symphony Orchestra, and the waterfront home tent of the world-famous Cirque du Soleil circus. In summer the city hosts popular events such as the Montreal International Jazz Festival and the Just for Laughs comedy festival. Museums include the Montreal Museum of Fine Arts and, on the site of the city's founding settlement, the Pointe-à-Callière Montreal Museum of Archaeology and History. Schoolchildren like to visit the Biodome—a living museum where four different

Montreal is a cultural mecca. The Montreal Museum of Fine Arts (left) *boasts a collection of fine artworks from many of the world's most famous artists. The Just for Laughs Festival* (above) *attracts visitors from all over the province.*

From inside the Biodome (above) *visitors can experience a walk through a rain forest and three other ecosystems.* (Below) *Shoppers can pick up fresh local produce from the Atwater Market.*

environments, including the St. Lawrence River marine ecosystem, are re-created.

On summer evenings, cars are bumper-to-bumper on downtown thoroughfares such as St. Catherine Street. Sidewalks are full of people on their way to a show or to one of the city's many restaurants. Montreal is a great place to eat. The bagels and smoked meat sandwiches on St. Lawrence Boulevard are famous. You can buy Peking duck in Chinatown, fresh fish, cheese, and vegetables at the Atwater Market, and croissants at neighborhood bakeries.

Montreal is also an enthusiastic sports city. Local fans support their favorite teams—the Montreal Canadiens hockey team and the Montreal Expos baseball team. The city also has professional soccer and football teams.

Hockey fans cheer on the red-white-and-blue Montreal Canadiens as they face off against their rivals.

Employment and Economy ▶ With two French-language and two English-language universities, Montreal is a center for high-technology industries. Many people are employed in information technology (such as software and telecommunications equipment) and the aeronautics, transportation equipment, and pharmaceutical fields. Food and beverage industries provide many other jobs. The headquarters of several large corporations in the engineering and transportation equipment fields are also located in Montreal. And the city is home to several international organizations, such as the International Civil Aviation Organization.

The largest source of jobs in the MUC is the service sector. Service jobs—including transportation, communications, government, education, medical, leisure and business services, real estate, and retail sales services—represent

77 percent of the MUC's economy. The manufacture of goods—such as machinery and transportation equipment, electronic products, paper and printed materials, textiles and clothing, chemicals, and food and beverages—provides 21 percent of employment. About 2 percent of the area's jobs are in construction and mining. Farms lie near the city but are located off the heavily built-up island. Agricultural employment, therefore, is not included in MUC statistics.

About one-fifth of Montreal's workers are employed in manufacturing.

Times are tough, however, and poverty and unemployment in the MUC are high. Manufacturing jobs in fields such as plastics, tobacco, and metal products have declined since the mid-1980s. Since the 1970s, many large banks and insurance companies have moved their head offices from Montreal to Toronto or to western Canada, leaving downtown offices vacant. Some business leaders do not want to invest in the city because of the possibility that Quebec might separate from Canada.

The Port of Montreal generates 1.2 billion Canadian dollars (U.S. $896 million) a year for the area economy, supporting about 7,400 port jobs. These include jobs in administration, rail and grain facilities, and stevedoring services, as well as jobs in port-related service companies, such as steamship agencies, customs offices, freight forwarding companies, marine law firms, insurance agencies, and marine supply companies. The port supports another 6,300 indirect jobs in businesses such as restaurants and banks that provide services to port-related industries.

However, the port creates far fewer jobs than it did before the arrival of the container era. Years ago ships were in port for several weeks, and crew members enjoyed recreation facilities near the waterfront. Nowadays ships turn around in two or three days or in as little as a matter of hours. Vessels used to undergo major repairs in Montreal, but the **dry dock** went out of business in 1988. Also, machines do most of the work that manual laborers once did to unload and reload ships. The port had about 3,000 dockworkers in the late 1960s when the first

> ▶ After high school, many young Quebecers attend junior colleges called CEGEPs. Sixty percent of CEGEP students take pre-university courses, and 40 percent enroll in professional and technical programs.
>
> ▶ Montreal has a circus school where performers aged 12 and older learn juggling and other circus skills.
>
> ▶ Membership in the longshoremen's, or dockworkers', union is frequently a family affair with fathers, sons, and brothers all working on the docks. A few women are also employed as dockworkers.
>
> ▶ Most Montreal dockworkers are Quebecois (French Quebecers). Except for a few workers of English descent, few other ethnic groups are represented on the docks.

container terminal opened. By the mid-1990s, the port supported only 760 dockworkers.

The dockworkers are employed by the Maritime Employers' Association, which brings together all the stevedoring companies and shipping lines in the port. The workers are sent out to different terminals each day, depending on which ones have ships in port. All the dockworkers make the same base salary, whether they are operating a gantry crane or stacking breakbulk cargo. They are guaranteed 40 hours of work each week and earn extra when they work nights and overtime.

The port may not provide as many jobs as it once did, but it still plays an important role in the region's economy. And although many Montrealers are more familiar with the Old Port's recreational facilities than with the cranes and containers of the working port, both assure Montreal's prominent place on the world map and its reputation as a good city in which to live and to work.

With container traffic on the increase and a wide range of state-of-the-art equipment, the Port of Montreal faces a bright future.

GLOSSARY

balance of trade: The difference over time between the value of a country's imports and its exports.

breakbulk cargo: A term used to refer to non-containerized general cargo. This cargo category includes items packaged in separate units, such as boxes, cases, and pallets, as well as heavy machinery that is too big to be transported in a container.

bulk cargo: Raw products, such as grains and minerals, that are not packaged in separate units. Dry bulk cargo is typically piled loosely in a ship's cargo holds, while liquid bulk cargo is piped into a vessel's storage tanks.

customs: Taxes or fees, such as duties and tolls, a nation places on imports and exports. Going through customs is the procedure for collecting such fees.

dry dock: A dock where a vessel is kept out of the water so that repairs can be made to the parts that lie below the water line.

gantry crane: A crane mounted on a platform supported by a framed structure that runs on parallel tracks so as to span or rise above a ship for purposes of loading and unloading heavy cargo.

general cargo: Cargo that is not shipped in bulk. This cargo category includes containerized and breakbulk cargo.

icebreaker: A powerful, heavy ship with a strengthened hull (body) that breaks through ice to maintain open, navigable channels of water. Some icebreakers ride on top of the ice until the weight of the vessel crushes the ice. Other ships break through the ice by backing up and ramming into it. The most powerful icebreakers can travel through ice that is more than 20 feet thick.

ice floe: A thick, flat piece of floating ice that has broken off from an ice shelf (a mass of coastal ice).

intermodal transportation: A system of transportation in which goods are moved from one type of vehicle to another, such as from a ship to a train or from a train to a truck, in the course of a single trip.

lock: An enclosed, water-filled chamber in a canal or river used to raise or lower boats beyond the site of a waterfall or a set of rapids. Vessels can enter and exit the lock through gates at either end.

TEU: Twenty-foot equivalent unit. Container traffic is measured in TEUs. One TEU represents a container that is 20 feet long, 8 feet wide, and 8.5 feet or 9.5 feet high.

PRONUNCIATION GUIDE

Cartier, Jacques	kahr-TYAY, ZHAHK
Champlain, Samuel de	shawn-PLAn, sah-mew-EHL duh
Cité du Havre	see-TAY doo AH-vruh
Huron	HYUHR-ahn
Île Sainte-Hélène	EEL SANT-ay-LEHN
Iroquois	IHR-uh-kwoy
Lachine	luh-SHEEN
Maisonneuve, Paul de Chomedey de	mehz-ohn-NUV, POHL duh shawm-DAY duh
Montreal	muhn-tree-AWL
Quebec	kwuh-BEHK

INDEX

Allan, Sir Hugh, 38–39
Arts and entertainment, 68–70
Atlantic Ocean, 7–8, 17, 51

Balance of trade, 58
Biodome, 69–70

Canadian Coast Guard, 17, 18, 44
Cargo, 12–15, 22–23, 53–57, 60
Cartier, Jacques, 28–29
Cast Terminal, 16
Champlain, Samuel de, 29–32
Cirque du Soleil, 68
Cité du Havre, 21
Containerized cargo, 13–15, 23–25, 44–47, 50, 52–53, 54, 73–74
Contrecoeur (Quebec), 47
Customs (payment of duties and taxes), 23, 61

Economy, 42–44, 46–47, 49–51, 59–61, 71–74
Education, 71, 73
Employment. *See* Jobs
Ethnic diversity, 67–68
Exports, 22, 36, 41, 42, 49–50, 52–53, 55, 56, 58, 59–60

Flooding, 37, 40, 44
Francophone (French-speaking) community, 67
Freight forwarders, 60–61
French explorers, 28–32
Fur trade, 30, 32–33

Future of the port, 45–47, 73–74

Gantry cranes, 13, 24–25
Grains, 12, 41, 56–57
Grands Ballets Canadiens, 68
Great Depression, 42
Great Lakes, 8, 17, 43, 57
Great Lakes-St. Lawrence Seaway System, 8, 17, 43, 57

History, 27–47; early peoples, 27–28; 1800s, 34–39; French explorers, 28–33; future of the port, 45–47, 73–74; 1900s, 40–42; port improvements, 40–45; St. Lawrence Seaway, 42–44
Hovercraft, 19

Iberville Passenger Terminal, 20–21
Icebreakers, 18, 19, 44
Île Sainte-Hélène (St. Helen's Island), 20
Imperial Oil wharf, 40
Imports, 41, 49–50, 52–53, 55–56, 58
Independence movement (Quebec's), 45–46
Industry, 44–45, 71–74
Intermodal transportation, 52–54
International Jazz Festival, 69
International trade, 49–61
Iroquois, 28, 32

Jacques Cartier Bridge, 16

Jacques Cartier Square, 63–64
Jobs, 42, 49, 71–74
Just for Laughs Festival, 69

Lachine Canal, 34–36
Lachine Rapids, 9, 31, 35, 36
Language, 67–68
Locks, 17, 35

Maisonneuve, Paul de Chomedey de, 32
maps, 2, 8, 10–11, 31, 66
Maritime Employers' Association, 74
Molson, John, 34
Montreal: ethnic diversity, 67–68; history, 27–48; jobs, 42, 49, 71–74 ; location and size, 7–11; maps, 10–11, 31, 66; population, 67
Montreal, Island of, 9, 16, 30–31, 46–47, 67
Montreal Port Corporation, 16, 22–23
Montreal Symphony Orchestra, 68
Montreal Urban Community (MUC), 67, 71–74
Mount Royal, 9, 64–65
Museums, 69–70

Navigation systems, 15–16
Newfoundland, 9, 50
New France, 30, 33
North American Free Trade Agreement (NAFTA), 59

Old Montreal, 29, 62–65
Old Port, 16, 20, 22, 45, 63, 74
Ontario, 7, 8, 47, 56
Ontario, Lake, 8, 9, 43

Petroleum products, 12, 15, 16–17, 21, 57
Population, 67
Port administration, 16, 22–23, 73
Port of Montreal, map of, 10–11
Port services, 21–22, 73–74

Quebec, 8, 45–46, 67, 73
Quebec City, 15, 30, 32, 33, 36–37, 53, 57

Racine Terminal, 23

Railroads. *See* Trains

St. Lawrence, Gulf of, 8–9, 37
St. Lawrence River, 7–8, 9, 15, 16, 18, 28–32, 35, 36–37, 42–43, 46, 51, 57, 67
St. Lawrence Seaway, 9, 17, 42–44, 57
St. Mary's Current, 20, 31
St. Pierre, Lake, 18, 29, 31–32, 33, 36
St. Pierre River, 30
Shipping, 12–16, 18–19, 23–25, 38, 42–44, 51–58, 60
Sports, 70–71
Steamships, 34, 36, 38

Tourism, 21

Trade, 12–15, 49–61
Trading houses, 59–60
Trains, 22, 23, 25, 36, 40, 47, 50, 53, 56
Transportation links, 21, 23, 25, 44, 50, 52–53, 60–61, 67

Underground City, 65
Unemployment, 73–74

Wars, 32–33, 40, 42
Wintertime navigation, 18–19, 37, 44–45
World Trade Organization, 59

Young, John, 27

METRIC CONVERSION CHART

WHEN YOU KNOW	MULTIPLY BY	TO FIND
inches	2.54	centimeters
feet	0.3048	meters
miles	1.609	kilometers
square feet	0.0929	square meters
square miles	2.59	square kilometers
acres	0.4047	hectares
pounds	0.454	kilograms
tons	0.9072	metric tons
bushels	0.0352	cubic meters
gallons	3.7854	liters

ABOUT THE AUTHOR

Janice Hamilton is a writer and freelance journalist who worked for several years in the Montreal bureau of The Canadian Press. As a freelancer, she covers a wide range of issues, from the environment to immigration laws. Her articles have appeared in a variety of publications, including the *Canadian Medical Association Journal* and *Canadian Geographic*. Ms. Hamilton has also written a Lerner title about the province of Quebec, where she lives with her husband and two sons.

ACKNOWLEDGMENTS

I would like to thank all those who helped me research this book, especially Michel Turgeon and Brent Frederick of the Port of Montreal. Without their patient cooperation, this project would have been impossible. I would also like to mention Normand Massicotte, who gave me a fascinating tour of the Racine Terminal, as well as Brian Slack of the geography department at Concordia University, Montreal, and Leo Ryan, editor of *Canadian Sailings,* who gave me fresh perspectives on the port. As for the historical material, I am indebted to a number of sources, including Kathleen Jenkins *(Montreal: Island City of the St. Lawrence)*, Edgar Andrew Collard *(Montreal: The Days that Are No More)* for his lively vignettes of the city's past, Raoul Blanchard *(Montréal: Esquisse de Géographie Urbaine)*, Paul-André Linteau *(Histoire de Montréal depuis la Confédération)*, and Stephen Leacock, the economist and humorist, whose *Montreal: Seaport and City* is a long out-of-print treasure.